MEET ALL THESE FRIENDS IN BUZZ BOOKS:

Thomas the Tank Engine
Fireman Sam
Bugs Bunny
Looney Tunes
Tiny Toon Adventures
Police Academy
Toucan 'Tecs
Flintstones
Jetsons
Joshua Jones

First published 1992 by Buzz Books,
an imprint of Reed International Books Ltd
Michelin House, Fulham Road, London SW3 6RB

LONDON   MELBOURNE   AUCKLAND

Text adapted from an original cartoon entitled
Dino Disappears

ISBN 1 85591 221 X

Printed and bound in the UK by BPCC Hazell Books

THE FLINTSTONES ™

IN

DINO'S DOUBLE

Story adapted by Caryn Jenner
from an original cartoon
Illustrations by Primary Design

"Well, that's another day's work over,"
said Fred as he and Barney drove home.
"I can't wait to get home to relax with Wilma
and Pebbles."

Fred slowed down to cross the bridge.

"Oh no," he said suddenly, glancing at the
string tied round his finger. "I knew I'd
forgotten something."

"Something for Pebbles, maybe?" Barney suggested.

"Yeah, that's it! Something for Pebbles," said Fred, smiling at the thought of his baby daughter.

AND YOU USUALLY DO, FRED.

At home, Wilma gave Dino a special bone.

"Happy anniversary, Dino," she said.

Pebbles clapped and Dino barked happily.

"You're such a big help in taking care of Pebbles," Wilma added. "You're just like one of the family, Dino."

Dino rushed to greet Fred at the door.

"Down boy," ordered Fred. He gave
Pebbles her gift. "Look what Daddy has
for you, Pebbles."

He rushed to set up the camera as Pebbles
cuddled her new doll.

"Didn't you get any dinosaur toys, Fred?"
Wilma asked.

"Why would I get dinosaur toys for
Pebbles?" Fred replied.

"Fred, how could you forget Dino's first anniversary with us?" Wilma asked later.

Fred snapped his fingers. "*That's* what the string was for."

"Yes, Fred, and you forgot anyway," said Wilma. "Why don't you apologise to Dino?"

OUT, DINO. NOW!

Dino was watching over Pebbles while she rocked happily in her cradle. Suddenly, Pebbles rocked a little too hard. The cradle tipped dangerously, and was about to topple over with Pebbles inside it when Dino leaped to the rescue and caught her in his mouth!

Fred entered just in time to see Dino grab Pebbles. "Dino, put Pebbles down!" he yelled. "This is the last straw. From now on, you sleep outside."

The next morning, Wilma went out to give Dino his breakfast. But Dino wasn't there.

Reluctantly, Fred searched the garden for Dino. "He's definitely gone," Fred declared. "Looks like he's run away."

Pebbles burst into tears.

"I'm sorry Dino, wherever you are," said Fred, a tear trickling down his cheek.

Meanwhile, Dino was wandering around
town looking for a new home.

Oh Pebbles, he thought sadly, *how I miss you.*

Pebbles refused to eat anything until Dino came home.

"We've looked everywhere," said Fred, arriving home with Barney. They'd driven around town searching for Dino.

"No luck, I'm afraid," said Barney, "but we did put an advert in the newspaper."

REWARD OFFERED
FOR LOST FAMILY PET NAMED DINO.
SIX FEET TALL, PURPLE WITH SPOTS.

Wilma sighed. "We've just got to find Dino. I don't know what we'll do without him."

Just then the doorbell rang. Three people stood at the door, all with dinosaurs looking exactly like Dino.

"Here's your pet," they all said as they entered. "Where's my reward?"

Fred looked at the three dinosaurs. Which was the real Dino?

But Pebbles had already solved the problem. She crawled past the three dinosaurs and burst into tears again.

So once more Fred and Barney went in search of Dino.

"Barney, look in that garden!" exclaimed Fred. "It's Dino. He's been kidnapped."

"Lots of dinosaurs around here are purple with spots," Barney pointed out.

The dinosaur growled at Fred.

"See Barney?" said Fred. "Dino's mad at me because I yelled at him."

Just then a man ran out of the house.

"Hey, you leave Rocky alone or I'll ring the police!" he shouted.

"That's my Dino," Fred declared. "And I want him back."

"I'm sorry gentlemen, but you must be mistaken," the man said. He turned to the dinosaur. "Rocky, show these two men the way out."

GOOD BOY, ROCKY.

At home, Fred made a plan.

"We've got to get Dino back, Barney. And I know how," he said.

"But Fred, I don't think that dinosaur was Dino," said Barney.

"'Course it was," Fred insisted. "I'll sleep in Dino's shed for a week if that wasn't Dino. Now listen Barney, this is what we're going to do..."

If only Fred had known that the real
Dino was still wandering the streets, hungry
and lonely.

Fred and Barney went back to the house where they'd seen the dinosaur.

"When I say 'now', you slip the sack over Dino's head and I'll grab him," Fred told Barney.

The plan worked perfectly until the dinosaur started howling.

"Be quiet, Dino," Fred whispered. "We've come to rescue you."

The dinosaur howled even louder, waking up his owner.

"Put my dinosaur down, you thieves!" the man cried. "Police! Help, police!"

Fred and Barney sped off in the car, with the dinosaur wriggling on Barney's lap.

"We did it!" Fred exclaimed.

But from a distance, Barney heard a siren rapidly gaining on them.

"Uh, Fred, sounds like the police behind us," he said.

YOU'RE UNDER ARREST FOR STEALING A PET DINOSAUR.

So what? All I did was take back my own pet dinosaur," Fred replied.

"I hope you're right," said Barney.

"I told you, if this dinosaur isn't Dino, I'll sleep in Dino's shed. That's how sure I am," Fred declared, as the police officer approached the car.

Wilma, Betty and Pebbles went down to the police station to bail out Fred. He was still trying to convince the angry owner that the dinosaur was really Dino.

"His name is Rocky and he's my dinosaur," the man retorted.

"Do you see that sweet little girl?" Fred asked. "She hasn't eaten a thing since you took Dino."

LOOK, THERE'S DINO! COME HERE, BOY.

Pebbles looked at Rocky and burst into tears. That wasn't her dinosaur!

Then, a miracle happened. Dino was wandering by the police station looking for a few morsels of food. He looked in the window and saw his precious Pebbles. He raced into the station.

Everyone was glad to have Dino home
again, even Fred.

"Gee Fred, when you make a bet, you
really go through with it," said Barney.

"A bargain is a bargain," said Fred.
"Besides, I've got to admit it - our Dino
is one in a million."